A NOTE TO PARENTS

Reading Aloud with Your Child

Research shows that reading books aloud is the single most valuable support parents can provide in helping children learn to read.

- Be a ham! The more enthusiasm you display, the more your child will enjoy the book.
- Run your finger underneath the words as you read to signal that the print carries the story.
- Leave time for examining the illustrations more closely; encourage your child to find things in the pictures.
- Invite your youngster to join in whenever there's a repeated phrase in the text.
- Link up events in the book with similar events in your child's life.
- If your child asks a question, stop and answer it. The book can be a means to learning more about your child's thoughts.

Listening to Your Child Read Aloud

The support of your attention and praise is absolutely crucial to your child's continuing efforts to learn to read.

- If your child is learning to read and asks for a word, give it immediately so that the meaning of the story is not interrupted. DO NOT ask your child to sound out the word.
- On the other hand, if your child initiates the act of sounding out, don't intervene.
- If your child is reading along and makes what is called a miscue, listen for the sense of the miscue. If the word "road" is substituted for the word "street," for instance, no meaning is lost. Don't stop the reading for a correction.
- If the miscue makes no sense (for example, "horse" for "house"), ask your child to reread the sentence because you're not sure you understand what's just been read.
- Above all else, enjoy your child's growing command of print and make sure you give lots of praise. *You are your child's first teacher—and the most important one. Praise from you is critical for further risk-taking and learning.*

—Priscilla Lynch
Ph.D., New York University
Educational Consultant

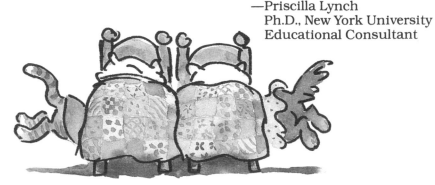

For my sisters and all the 'S' cats
—S. K.

To Dundee and Bones
—B. L.

Text copyright © 1993 by Stephen Krensky.
Illustrations copyright © 1993 by Betsy Lewin.
All rights reserved. Published by Scholastic Inc.
CARTWHEEL BOOKS is a trademark of Scholastic Inc.
HELLO READER! is a registered trademark of Scholastic Inc.

Library of Congress Cataloging-in-Publication Data

Krensky, Stephen.
   Fraidy Cats / by Stephen Krensky : illustrated by Betsy Lewin.
      p.   cm.—(Hello reader)
   "Cartwheel book."
   Summary: One dark and noisy night the Fraidy Cats let their imaginations run wild, visualizing scary things from wild elephants to hungry wolves.
   ISBN 0-590-46438-8
   [1. Cats—Fiction.   2. Fear of the dark—Fiction.   3. Night—Fiction. 4. Bedtime—Fiction.]   I. Lewin, Betsy, ill.   II. Title.   III. Series.
PZ8.3.K869Fr   1993
[E]—dc20
                                                                            92-35360
                                                                                CIP
                                                                                 AC
12   11   10   9   8   7   6   5   4   3   2   1   3   4   5   6   7   8/9
                        Printed in the U.S.A.   23
            First Scholastic printing, September 1993

FRAIDY CATS

by Stephen Krensky • Illustrated by Betsy Lewin

Hello Reader!—Level 2

SCHOLASTIC INC.
Cartwheel ·B·O·O·K·S·™

New York   London   Toronto   Sydney   Auckland

One dark night
when the wind blew hard,
the Fraidy Cats got ready for bed.
Scamper checked in the closet.
Nothing was there.
Sorry checked under the beds.
Nothing there, either.

They checked behind the curtains
and the door.
All was well.
They crawled into their beds
and fixed the covers.
"Good night," said Scamper.
"Pleasant dreams," said Sorry.
Then they heard a noise.

TAP, TAP, TAP!
"I hear a dog," said Sorry.
"A big hairy dog."
"Is it friendly?" Scamper asked.

"No," said Sorry.
"It likes to chase cats."
She jumped up
and shut the door.

HISSSSS!
"I hear a snake," said Scamper.
"It scared the dog away."
"Is it a cute little garden snake?"
Sorry asked.

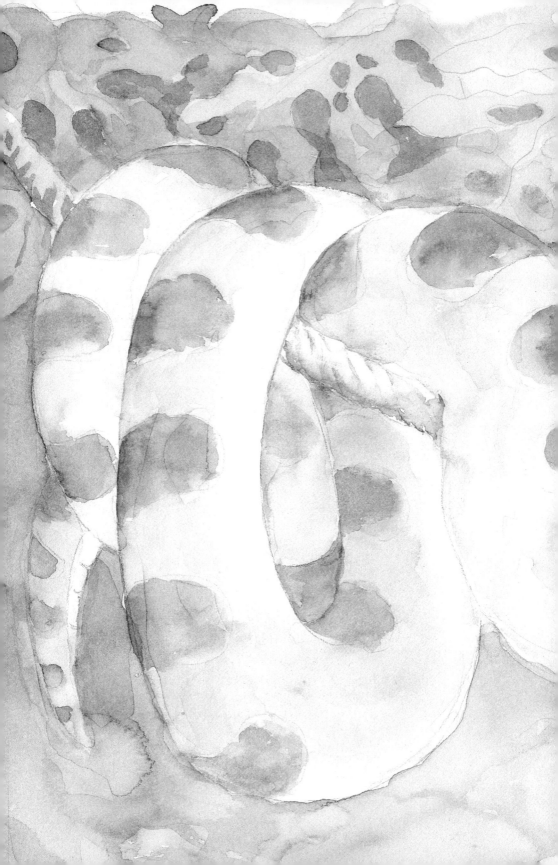

"No," said Scamper,
"It's a long giant snake
— and it hasn't eaten in a week."
He got up
and pushed a blanket
in the crack under the door.

SCREECH!
"I hear an eagle," said Sorry.
"It scared the snake away."
"Is it a gentle baby eagle?"
asked Scamper.

Sorry shook her head.
"It's a fierce mountain eagle,
swooping down from the clouds
to carry something back
to its rocky nest."
She ran to the window
and shut it.

WOOO! WOOO!
"I hear a wolf," said Scamper.
"It scared the eagle away."
"Is this a wolf that only likes to eat
three little pigs?" asked Sorry.

"Oh, no," said Scamper.
"This is a wolf
with many sharp teeth.
It will eat almost anything it sees."
He ran to the window
and shut the curtains.

ROOOORRR!
"I hear an elephant," said Sorry.
"It scared the wolf away."

"Is this a tame elephant
that ran away from the circus?"
Scamper asked.

"No," said Sorry.
"This is a wild elephant
with legs like tree trunks.
It crushes things that get in its way."
Scamper and Sorry
looked at each other
and dove under their beds.

BOOM! BOOM!
"I hear a dinosaur," said Scamper.
"It scared the elephant away."
"Is this a small dinosaur
the size of a lizard?" Sorry asked.
Scamper bit his lip.
"It is as big as a house," he said.

"And there's nothing left to close
or lock or hide under.
We can't stop it."
Sorry poked her head out.
"Wait a minute," she said.
"What kind of dinosaur is it?"
Scamper wasn't sure.

BOOM! BOOM! BOOM!
The room shook.
The windows rattled.
"It must be an ultrasaurus," said Sorry.
"The biggest, heaviest dinosaur
that ever lived.
We're doomed."

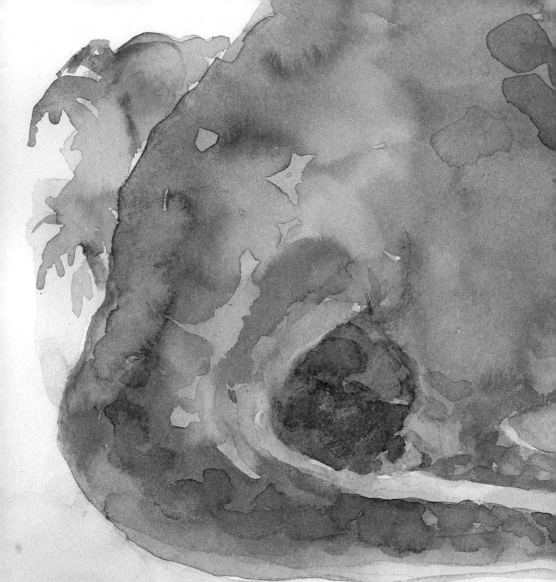

Scamper frowned.
"Wait a minute. I've read about
ultrasaurs. They only ate plants."
"Are you sure?"
"Positive."
"No cats?"
Scamper shook his head.

Sorry smiled.
"Then the ultrasaurus
will stay in the garden."
"And, it will scare away anything
else that comes by," said Scamper.
"We're safe at last."

The night was still dark.
The wind still blew hard.
The Fraidy Cats didn't care.
They got back into bed
and fixed the covers.
"Good night!" they said together,
and then fell fast asleep.